TEENAGE MUTANT NINJA TURTLES

NEW ANIMATED ADVENTURES

VOLUME 4

STORY: ERIK BURNHAM

ART: DARIO BRIZUELA

COLORS: HEATHER BRECKEL

LETTERS: SHAWN LEE

EDITS: BOBBY CURNOW

 Spotlight

ABDOPUBLISHING.COM

Reinforced library bound edition published in 2016 by Spotlight, a division of ABDO
PO Box 398166, Minneapolis, Minnesota 55439. Spotlight produces high-quality
reinforced library bound editions for schools and libraries.
Published by agreement with IDW.

Printed in the United States of America, North Mankato, Minnesota.
092015
012016

THIS BOOK CONTAINS
RECYCLED MATERIALS

CATALOGING-IN-PUBLICATION DATA

Byerly, Kenny.
 Teenage Mutant Ninja Turtles : new animated adventures / writer, Kenny Byerly ; illustrator, Dario
Brizuela. -- Reinforced library bound edition.
  p. cm. (Teenage Mutant Ninja Turtles : new animated adventures)
Volumes 1-2 written by Kenny Byerly ; illustrated by Dario Brizuela. -- Volume 3 written by Scott
Tipton, David Tipton, and Kenny Byerly ; illustrated by Dario Brizuela. -- Volume 4 written by Erik
Burnham ; illustrated by Dario Brizuela.
Summary: Spinning straight out of the hit Nickelodeon show, a fantastic tale takes the Turtles on a
dangerous rescue mission.
ISBN 978-1-61479-459-2 (vol. 1) -- ISBN 978-1-61479-460-8 (vol. 2) -- ISBN 978-1-61479-461-5
(vol. 3) -- ISBN 978-1-61479-462-2 (vol. 4)
1. Teenage Mutant Ninja Turtles (Fictitious characters)--Juvenile fiction.
2. Superheroes--Juvenile fiction. 3. Adventure and adventurers--Juvenile fiction. 4. Graphic
novels--Juvenile fiction. I. Brizuela, Dario, illustrator. II. Tipton, Scott, author. III. Tipton, David,
author. IV. Burnham, Erik, author. V. Title.
741.5--dc23

2015955128

Spotlight

A Division of ABDO
abdopublishing.com

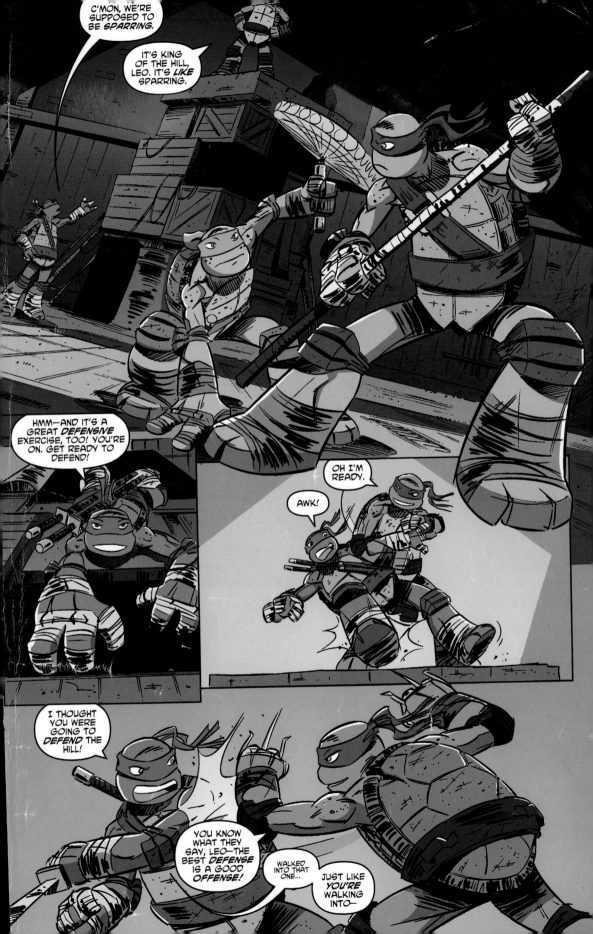

MEANWHILE...

YOUR BACK IS NOT STRAIGHT.

IT *CAN'T GET* ANY STRAIGHTER!

"*CAN'T*"? NEXT YOU WILL TELL ME THAT FOUR MUTATED TURTLES CAN'T BECOME MASTERS OF NINJUTSU.

MASTER SPLINTER!

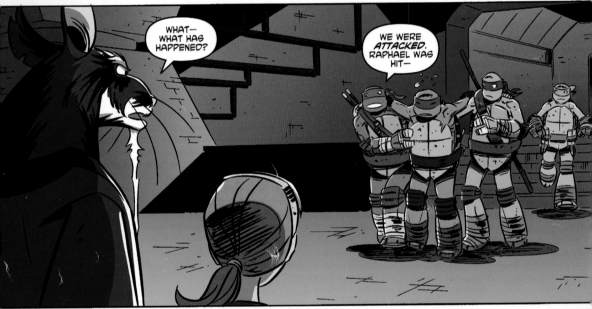

WHAT— WHAT HAS HAPPENED?

WE WERE *ATTACKED*. RAPHAEL WAS HIT—

—BY ONE OF *THESE*.

CHILK

WHAT IS IT, SENSEI?

POISON, MY SON. ONE I HAD THOUGHT *LOST.*

SNIFF SNIFF

OKAY, ALL THAT'S LEFT TO GET IS THE KYOSUU FRUIT, AND THIS IS THE ONLY OTHER PLACE SPLINTER THINKS IT WOULD BE... SO LET'S *FIND IT* AND GET HOME. THE CLOCK IS *TICKING.*

OKAY, WAIT, WHAT DOES THIS KYOSUU STUFF LOOK LIKE AGAIN?

SERIOUSLY, MIKEY? I TOLD YOU AT THE LAST PLACE!

I WAS DISTRACTED BY A PINEAPPLE-AND-KIELBASA FROZEN PIZZA. I'M NOT MADE OF *STONE,* DUDE. AND BESIDES—

—THIS PLACE HAS A *LOT* OF FRUIT!

SIGH. IT *LOOKS* LIKE A LEMON. A STRIPED LEMON. THAT CAN'T BE HARD TO MISS.

STRIPES, HUH? HERE'S ONE WITH POLKA DOTS...

...WAIT, NO, THAT'S MOLD.

HEY! I GOT ONE!